PLEASANT VALLEY FREE LIBRARY

W9-DCJ-619

The Twisted Fairy Tale

Written by
Elena Tait

Illustrated by
Christen Prete

AuthorHouse™
1663 Liberty Drive, Suite 200
Bloomington, IN 47403
www.authorhouse.com
Phone: 1-800-839-8640

©2009 Elena Tait. All rights reserved.

No part of this book may be reproduced, stored in a retrieval system, or transmitted by any means without the written permission of the author.

First published by AuthorHouse   1/26/2009

ISBN: 978-1-4389-2774-9 (sc)

Printed in the United States of America
Bloomington, Indiana

This book is printed on acid-free paper.

authorHOUSE®

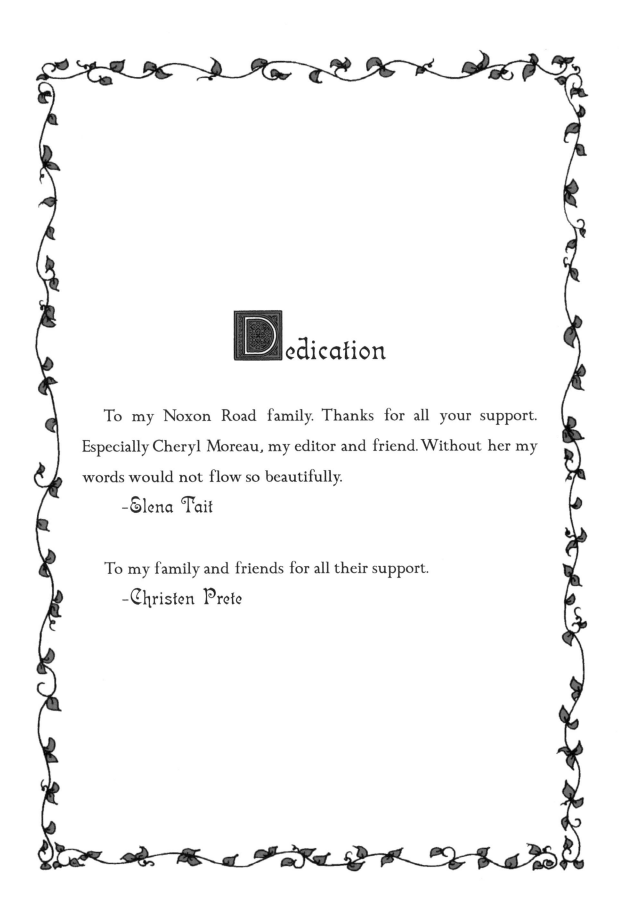

Dedication

To my Noxon Road family. Thanks for all your support. Especially Cheryl Moreau, my editor and friend. Without her my words would not flow so beautifully.

-Elena Tait

To my family and friends for all their support.

-Christen Prete

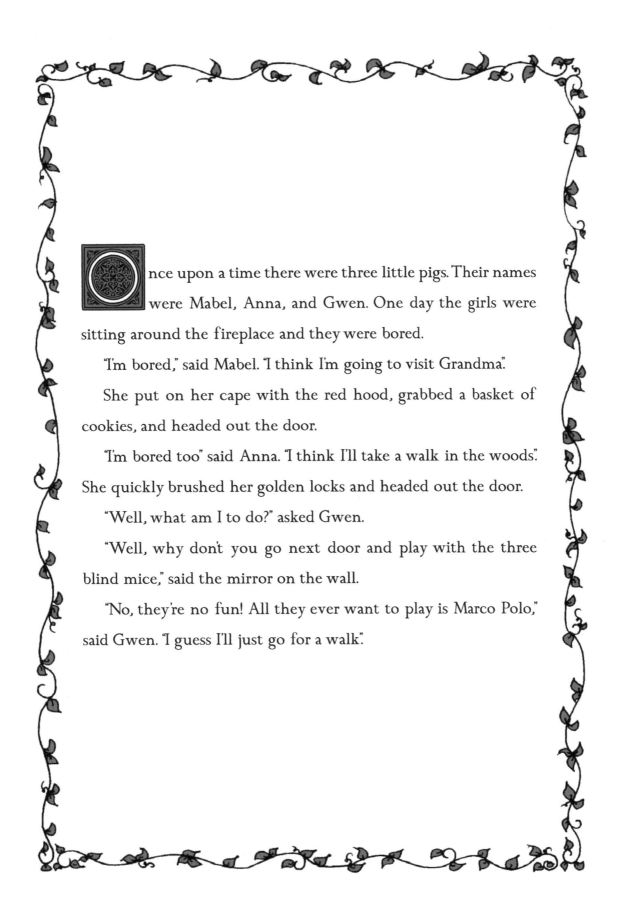

Once upon a time there were three little pigs. Their names were Mabel, Anna, and Gwen. One day the girls were sitting around the fireplace and they were bored.

"I'm bored," said Mabel. "I think I'm going to visit Grandma."

She put on her cape with the red hood, grabbed a basket of cookies, and headed out the door.

"I'm bored too" said Anna. "I think I'll take a walk in the woods." She quickly brushed her golden locks and headed out the door.

"Well, what am I to do?" asked Gwen.

"Well, why don't you go next door and play with the three blind mice," said the mirror on the wall.

"No, they're no fun! All they ever want to play is Marco Polo," said Gwen. "I guess I'll just go for a walk."

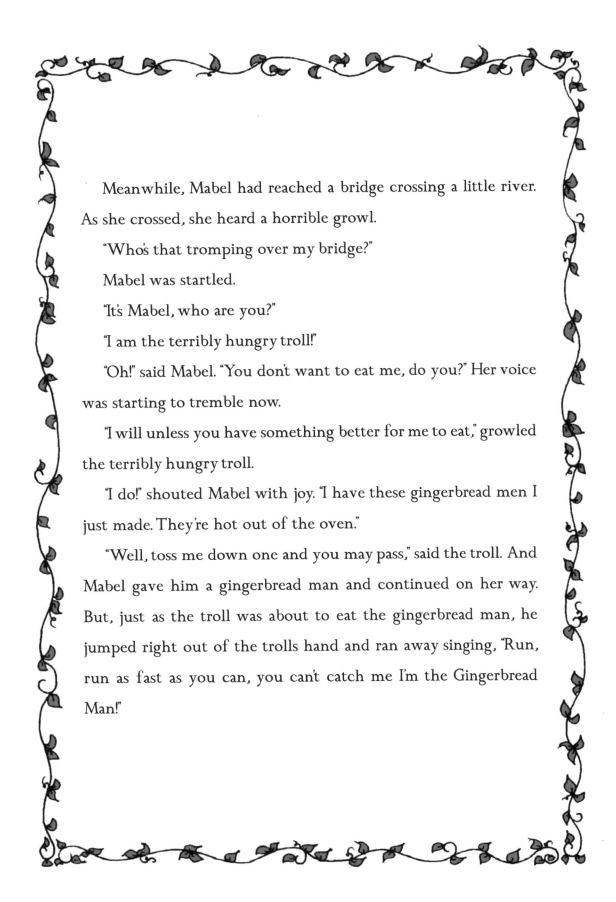

Meanwhile, Mabel had reached a bridge crossing a little river. As she crossed, she heard a horrible growl.

"Who's that tromping over my bridge?"

Mabel was startled.

"It's Mabel, who are you?"

"I am the terribly hungry troll!"

"Oh!" said Mabel. "You don't want to eat me, do you?" Her voice was starting to tremble now.

"I will unless you have something better for me to eat," growled the terribly hungry troll.

"I do!" shouted Mabel with joy. "I have these gingerbread men I just made. They're hot out of the oven."

"Well, toss me down one and you may pass," said the troll. And Mabel gave him a gingerbread man and continued on her way. But, just as the troll was about to eat the gingerbread man, he jumped right out of the trolls hand and ran away singing, "Run, run as fast as you can, you can't catch me I'm the Gingerbread Man!"

Now, on the other side of the woods, Anna was enjoying a nice stroll when she suddenly came upon a cottage. She peeked in the windows to see if anyone was home. The house looked empty but on the table she spotted some oatmeal cooling in bowls. She was very hungry and decided to go in and have just a small bite. She went around to the front door and found that it was unlocked. She crept inside and sat down in front of the first bowl. She tasted it and it was too hot, so she tried the next one. It was too cold, so she tried the smallest bowl. That one was just right, so she finished it all up.

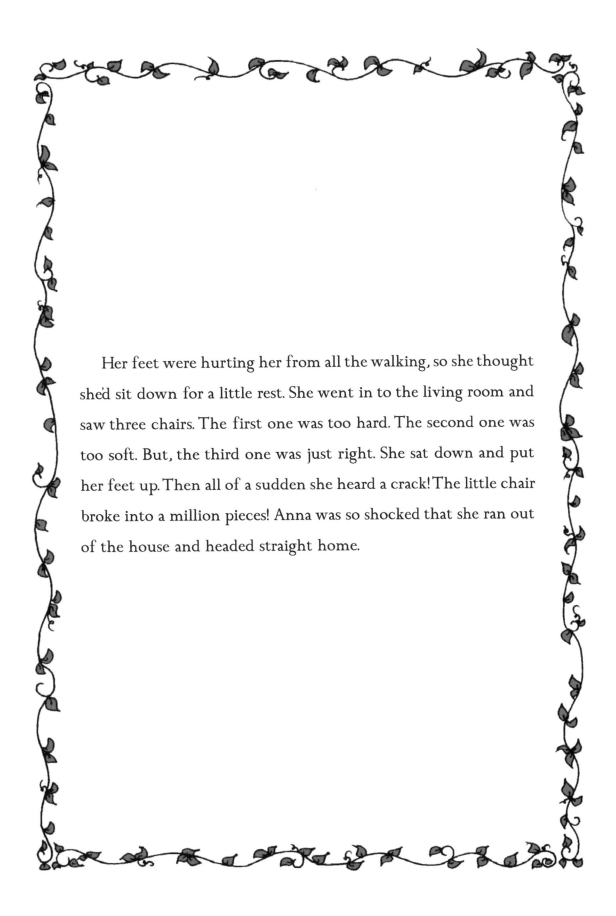

Her feet were hurting her from all the walking, so she thought she'd sit down for a little rest. She went in to the living room and saw three chairs. The first one was too hard. The second one was too soft. But, the third one was just right. She sat down and put her feet up. Then all of a sudden she heard a crack! The little chair broke into a million pieces! Anna was so shocked that she ran out of the house and headed straight home.

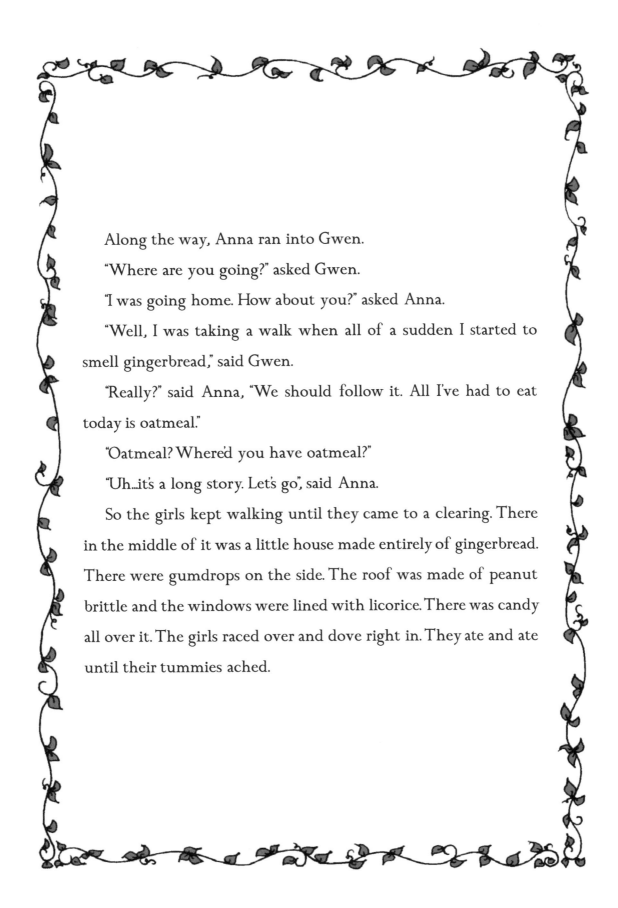

Along the way, Anna ran into Gwen.

"Where are you going?" asked Gwen.

"I was going home. How about you?" asked Anna.

"Well, I was taking a walk when all of a sudden I started to smell gingerbread," said Gwen.

"Really?" said Anna, "We should follow it. All I've had to eat today is oatmeal."

"Oatmeal? Where'd you have oatmeal?"

"Uh...it's a long story. Let's go", said Anna.

So the girls kept walking until they came to a clearing. There in the middle of it was a little house made entirely of gingerbread. There were gumdrops on the side. The roof was made of peanut brittle and the windows were lined with licorice. There was candy all over it. The girls raced over and dove right in. They ate and ate until their tummies ached.

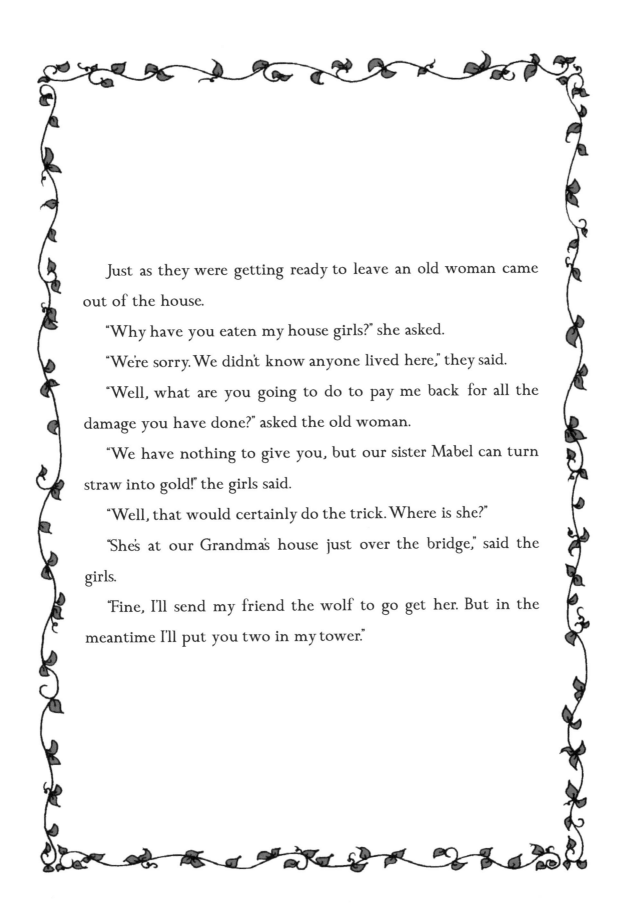

Just as they were getting ready to leave an old woman came out of the house.

"Why have you eaten my house girls?" she asked.

"We're sorry. We didn't know anyone lived here," they said.

"Well, what are you going to do to pay me back for all the damage you have done?" asked the old woman.

"We have nothing to give you, but our sister Mabel can turn straw into gold!" the girls said.

"Well, that would certainly do the trick. Where is she?"

"She's at our Grandma's house just over the bridge," said the girls.

"Fine, I'll send my friend the wolf to go get her. But in the meantime I'll put you two in my tower."

The wolf tromped through the forest to Grandma's house to retrieve Mabel. When he arrived Mabel was eating lunch with her grandmother. He grabbed her and stuffed her in a sack and dragged her back to the old lady's house.

"Your sisters have told me that you can spin straw into gold. You will be locked in my barn until you can spin me enough gold to pay for what your sisters have stolen from me!" screamed the old lady to a bewildered Mabel.

Mabel was thrown in the barn. There in front of her was the largest pile of straw she had ever seen. She began to cry for she had no idea how to spin straw into gold. "Oh what am I to do?" she cried.

A little elf walking by heard her crying and stopped in to see what was wrong. "Are you alright miss?"

"No, I'm not! I have to spin all this straw into gold and I don't know how!" cried Mabel.

"Well, I can do it for you," said the elf.

"You can?! I would be so very grateful. What could I give you in return?"

"You have to promise me your first born child" said the elf.

"Done!" shouted Mabel. And with that the elf set to work.

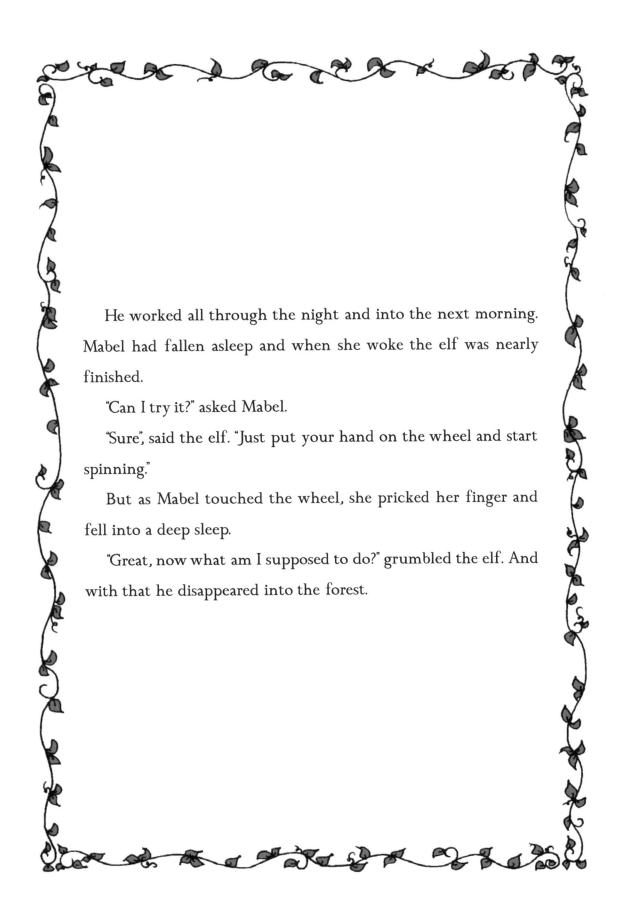

He worked all through the night and into the next morning.
Mabel had fallen asleep and when she woke the elf was nearly
finished.

"Can I try it?" asked Mabel.

"Sure", said the elf. "Just put your hand on the wheel and start
spinning."

But as Mabel touched the wheel, she pricked her finger and
fell into a deep sleep.

"Great, now what am I supposed to do?" grumbled the elf. And
with that he disappeared into the forest.

So while Mabel slept in the barn, Anna and Gwen were trying to find a way out of the tower. Days went by and nobody came for them. The little old lady had her gold. She took it and moved to Far, Far From Anywhere.

So the girls just sat there day and night. Nothing ever happened except that Gwen's hair started to grow and grow. It finally grew long enough that Anna was able to climb down it and leave the tower. But when she went to try to let Gwen out, she found the door was locked.

"Don't worry; I'll go get the woodsman to cut the lock with his ax!" Anna shouted up to Gwen. And with that, she ran off into the woods.

Gwen was so bored that she would sit in the window and sing for hours. Finally her singing paid off.

"Hello up there!" said a little boy goat.

"Hello! My name is Gwen. Can you get me down from here?"

"I can try. My name is Jack. Let me see if there's a ladder around."

So Jack ran all the way around the tower looking for a ladder. He didn't find one.

"Well?" asked Gwen.

"Nothing, but I have some beans! They're supposed to be magic, maybe they can help." So Jack planted the beans and stood back. He and Gwen held their breath and watched as a little plant began to grow. It grew bigger and taller, and bigger and taller, until it was right at Gwen's window. She climbed out onto the stalk and down to the ground.

"Thank you so much! I didn't think I was ever getting out of there!"

All of a sudden the ground began to shake and a terrible voice could be heard from up above. "FE FI FO FUM! Whose beanstalk just crashed through my aquarium?!"

As Gwen and Jack were looking up at a huge giant making his way down the stalk, Anna and the woodsman arrived to try to rescue Gwen.

"Hey, you got out!" shouted Anna.

"Yea, Jack got me out with his beanstalk, but now there's a giant coming down and he sounds mad!" said Gwen.

"Don't worry, I'll take care of this!" shouted the woodsman as he raised his ax and started chopping down the beanstalk.

CHOP, CHOP, CHOP! The ax cut its way through the beanstalk. With the final chop the beanstalk came down; and the giant with it. BOOM! The giant landed right on the tower, crumbling it to the ground. The girls, Jack and the woodsman took off running into the forest before the giant could get them.

They kept running until they got to the gingerbread house. They went to the barn to get Mabel but found her asleep in a glass box. There were seven little men sitting in front of the box crying.

"What happened to our sister?" asked Anna.

"She pricked her finger on the spinning wheel and fell into a deep sleep," answered one of the little men.

"Well, who are you?" asked Gwen.

"I am Plop and these are my brothers. We worked for the little old lady who lived here. We would go into the candy mines and get the candy she needed for her house."

"Did you put Mabel in that box?" asked Anna.

"Yes, we came by last week with a load of gumdrops and the old lady wasn't here. So, we looked around and found your sister asleep on the ground. She's so beautiful we put her in this glass box to protect her. We've been sitting here ever since."

"Well, how do we wake her up?" asked Gwen.

"She needs the kiss of a true king," said Doc.

"Are any of you kings?" asked Gwen. The dwarves, Jack, and the woodsman all shook their head no.

"There is a way to test it," Plop said.

"How?" Anna and Gwen asked excitedly.

"Behind the barn is a large stone. Stuck in the stone is a sword. Anyone who pulls it out will be king of all the land," replied Plop.

"Well, let's go try!" exclaimed Jack. The dwarves led Jack and the woodsman behind the barn. They each in turn climbed up on the stone and tried pulling the sword out. It wouldn't budge for the dwarves. It wouldn't budge for Jack. The woodsman climbed on the stone.

"Good luck, Woodsman!" cried out Anna.

"Please call me Arthur," the woodsman called back. And with that he pulled on the sword with all his might. The sword lifted out of the stone like it had been stuck in butter. Everyone cheered. The dwarves bowed down and everyone shouted, "All hail King Arthur!"

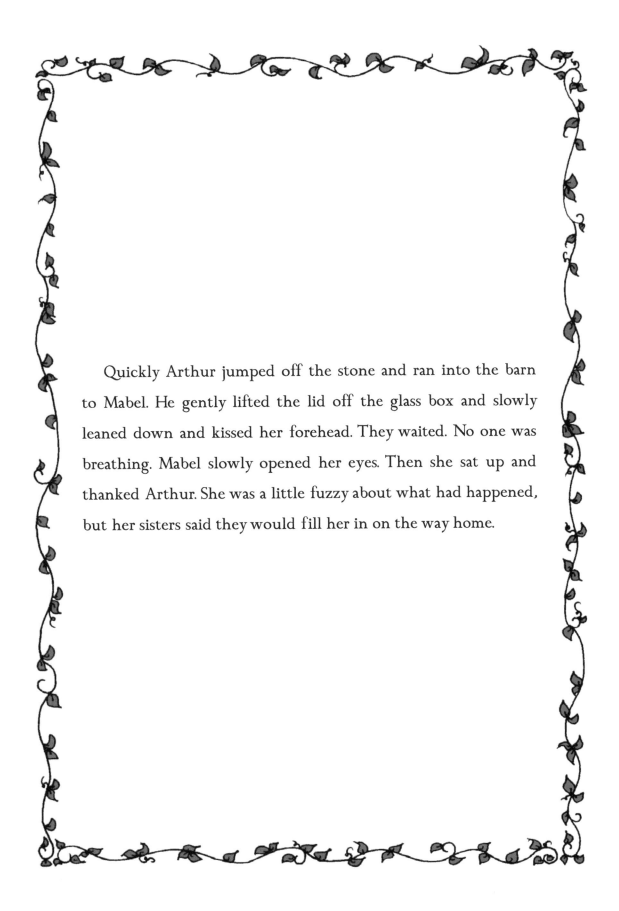

Quickly Arthur jumped off the stone and ran into the barn to Mabel. He gently lifted the lid off the glass box and slowly leaned down and kissed her forehead. They waited. No one was breathing. Mabel slowly opened her eyes. Then she sat up and thanked Arthur. She was a little fuzzy about what had happened, but her sisters said they would fill her in on the way home.

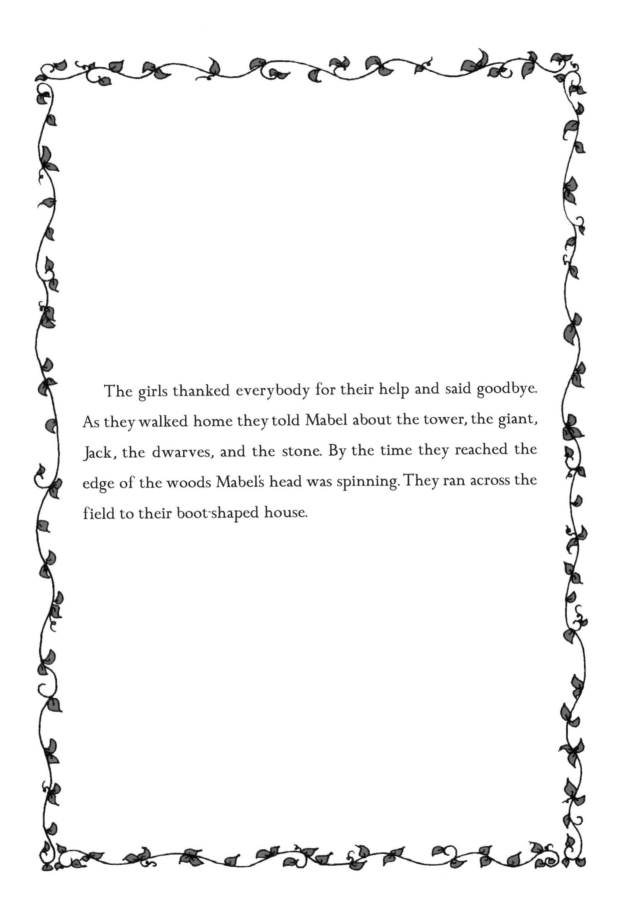

The girls thanked everybody for their help and said goodbye. As they walked home they told Mabel about the tower, the giant, Jack, the dwarves, and the stone. By the time they reached the edge of the woods Mabel's head was spinning. They ran across the field to their boot-shaped house.

As they walked in the back door they saw their mother sitting by the fire knitting.

"Oh Mother, Mother wait 'til we tell you about the adventures we had!" the girls shouted.

"Oh, my girls! I've been so worried about you. You've been gone for so long. Your father and his friend the donkey went looking for you days ago. Why don't you get some rest and tell me all about it in the morning." And she wrapped her wings around her three little girls and carried them up to bed.

Printed in the United States
140466LV00002B